SEAL OF THE FIRST CAT OF THE UNITED STATES

For August —C.B.

For Kai, Nonie, Zadie, and Stormy the cat —N.D.

Balzer + Bray is an imprint of HarperCollins Publishers.

The White House Cat
Text copyright © 2022 by Cylin Busby
Illustrations copyright © 2022 by Neely Daggett
All rights reserved. Manufactured in Italy.
No part of this book may be used or reproduced in any manner whatsoever without written
permission except in the case of brief quotations embodied in critical articles and reviews.
For information address HarperCollins Children's Books, a division of HarperCollins
Publishers, 195 Broadway, New York, NY 10007.
www.harpercollinschildrens.com
ISBN 978-0-06-313886-5

The artist used Adobe Photoshop and Procreate
to create the digital illustrations for this book.
Typography by Carla Weise
Hand lettering by Laura Mock
21 22 23 24 25 RTLO 10 9 8 7 6 5 4 3 2 1
❖
First Edition

The WHITE HOUSE CAT

Written by **Cylin Busby**

Illustrated by **Neely Daggett**

BALZER + BRAY
An Imprint of HarperCollinsPublishers

You've probably heard about the President and the First Lady.

You may have even heard about a few dogs who have lived at the White House. But what about the First Cat? Come with me and I'll show you who really runs things here—try to keep up!

My day starts early.

There's so much to do.

First stop: the kitchen, of course.
The pastry chef needs me to sample
the whipped cream. I'm happy to help.

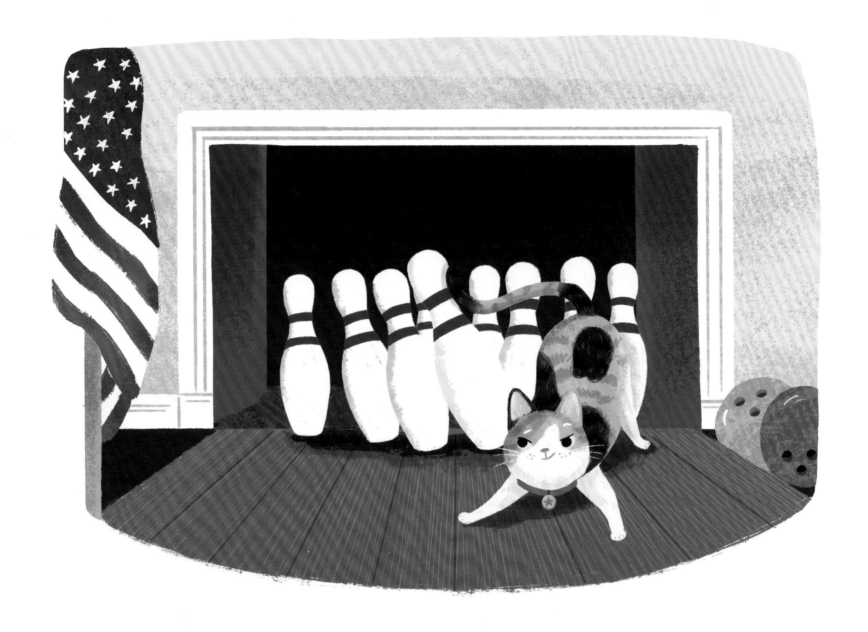

Then a shortcut through the bowling alley.
Another lucky strike!

The chief engineer and I check all the
moving bits and parts. She's a cat person.

The chief usher? Not so much.

I have to watch over the morning deliveries.
You never know when an uninvited guest might show up . . .

. . . and need a little help finding their way

to the Rose Garden.

Back inside for a quick inspection of the color rooms.

These curtains just won't
do what I tell them!

Behave!

The sparkly light in the Blue Room always keeps me on my paws.

It takes a steady tail to cross
the China Room.

I've never been a big fan of the art here anyway.

The piano keys seem
to be in tune, but let's test
them one more time.
It's hard to believe
those silly birds have been
holding this thing up for
years and years!

Getting this house in order is *a lot* of work.
Maybe I have time for just a little nap . . .

Or maybe not.

On my way through the West Wing, I always stop to see the latest news.

Front page? Nice.

Finally, to the Oval Office. Sorry I'm late!

Everyone is happy to see me.

Well, almost everyone . . .

A final check and all my duties are done.

Just
in
time . . .

Our VIPs—Very Important Pupils—are here!

There are a lot of things in the White House that say DON'T TOUCH.

I'm not one of them.

Now it's time to get some rest, because the day starts early at the White House, especially for me—the First Cat.

The White House (SOUTH VIEW)

PRESIDENT'S BEDROOM

RED ROOM

KITCHEN

STATE DINING ROOM

ENGINEERS' SHOP

TO THE WEST WING & OVAL OFFICE

THE ROSE GARDEN

SOUTH PATIO

FUN FACTS ABOUT THE WHITE HOUSE

Notes on page 3:

Our first president, George Washington, never lived in the **White House**! Construction began in 1792. Most of the laborers who built the White House were African Americans (both enslaved and freed); others were Irish, Scottish, and European immigrants. The White House wasn't ready for occupants until 1800, and the first president to actually live there was John Adams with his wife, Abigail. But since then, every US president has lived in the White House.

The present-day White House boasts 132 rooms, 35 bathrooms, 6 levels, 412 doors, 147 windows, 28 fireplaces, 8 staircases, and 3 elevators in addition to 30,000 historical objects (furniture, paintings, etc.).

Notes on pages 4-5:

The White House has 3 **kitchens** and 5 full-time chefs, including 1 pastry chef. The chefs are on duty 24 hours a day, 7 days a week, in case the president or a member of his family requests a snack. For the Easter Egg Roll and hunt every year, the chefs hard-boil and dye 14,000 eggs. The kitchen can serve dinner to 140 guests at one time, or hors d'oeuvres to 1,000.

The **bowling alley** was originally built under the West Wing (in the current Situation Room) but in 1969, President Richard M. Nixon, an avid bowler, had it relocated to the ground floor of the main residence, probably so that he could bowl more often!

Notes on pages 6-7:

When President Bill Clinton lived in the White House, his family's cat, Socks, loved to visit the **Engineers' Shop** on the lower level and became good friends with the chief engineer. In fact, the cat's permanent bed was in the Engineers' Shop. The Clintons also had a dog named Buddy, but sadly Socks and Buddy did not get along—at all!

The **chief usher** is an important job in the White House. The title comes from a time long ago when the usher's job was to "usher" the public in to see the president and first lady. Now the chief usher is in charge of the entire staff that runs the house, from the cooks and housekeepers to the plumbers and engineers.

Notes on pages 8-9:

The famous **Rose Garden** is a beautiful outdoor space that measures 125 feet long by 60 feet wide. Though it seems unbelievable now, up until the early 1900s this area was used to house stables for horses and carriages. First Lady Edith Roosevelt redesigned the space into a proper garden in 1902 and planted rose bushes that are still there today. Now the Rose Garden is typically used for White House media events, such as outdoor press conferences and receiving national heroes and sports teams. In 1961, President John F. Kennedy greeted the Project Mercury astronauts in the garden shortly after his wife, First Lady Jackie Kennedy, had redesigned it.

Notes on pages 10-11:

There are four **"color rooms"** in the White House that are named based on the color of their walls and furniture. They are the **Blue Room**, the **Green Room**, the **Red Room**, and the **Yellow Room**. Most of the furnishings in these rooms are original to the White House and have been there for hundreds of years. For example, the marble table in the Blue Room was purchased by President James Monroe and has been in the White House since 1817. The French chandelier that hangs over it is also from the nineteenth century.

Each floor of the White House residency has an oval-shaped room: the Diplomatic Reception Room on the lower level, the Blue Room on the first floor, and the Yellow Room above that. We'll see why those rooms were built round instead of square when we get to the Oval Office.

Notes on pages 12-13:

The **China Room** is where all the fancy dining plates, cups, and bowls for the White House are on display. Almost every administration that has lived in the White House has commissioned a full china service. Some of the pieces in this room are 150 years old! The plates and other service  ware are displayed chronologically, with the oldest pieces on the east side of the room. Both President Jimmy Carter and President Ronald Reagan enjoyed using the Lincoln purple-banded solferino porcelain for state dinners—imagine eating off the same plate that President Lincoln once had his dinner on! Hanging on one wall of the China Room is a huge oil painting of First Lady Grace Coolidge with her beloved collie, Rob Roy, commissioned in 1924.

Notes on pages 14-15:

In 1938, Theodore Steinway himself presented President Franklin D. Roosevelt with the golden eagle **Steinway Grand** that now sits in the White House Entrance Hall. This piano replaced another gilded instrument from 1903 (that piano is now in the Smithsonian Institution). Built especially for the White House, the golden eagle Steinway piano is held up by "legs" that are really three massive, carved, gilded American eagles. The piano was repaired once in 1979 and is still played during social functions, especially by members of the US military bands.

Notes on pages 16-17:

There are 28 **fireplaces** in the White House. Under President Martin Van Buren, there was a full-time position of "fire man" on the staff whose job was to stoke the furnace and keep all the fireplaces burning to warm the large mansion in the winter months before central heating. The fire man slept in the room that is now known as the China Room—this was before the White House had much of a porcelain collection to display.

Notes on pages 18-19:

The **West Wing** of the White House, like the Rose Garden, was actually a stable for horses and a storage area (for ice and wood) until the early 1900s. In 1902, President Theodore Roosevelt decided to permanently move his office to this area, to a space that is still called the Roosevelt Room—or sometimes called the Fish Room because Roosevelt kept an aquarium and several mounted fish in his office! The Executive Offices for the President as well as the press offices are all in the West Wing, along with the Brady Briefing Room, a small theater that you may see on TV when the press secretary gives daily briefings.

Notes on page 20-21:

The **Oval Office** isn't just famous for being the Executive Office of the President—it also has an interesting history and a reason for being round instead of square. Like the oval rooms in the residency, the Oval Office is a throwback to the early days of this country, when what we now call the United States was just a handful of British colonies. President Washington retained an old British tradition of receiving visitors in a formal reception called a "levee." Guests attending a levee would stand in a circle and the president could move around the room, greeting each one in turn. When the White House was built, several rooms were designed specifically for just this type of meeting—including the Oval Office.

Since it was presented to President Rutherford B. Hayes in 1880, the **Resolute Desk** has been used by every president except for three (Andrew Johnson, Nixon, and Gerald Ford). The desk was built from the timbers of the British ship the HMS *Resolute* and presented as a gift to the United States by Queen Victoria. The panel at the front of the desk was added by President Franklin Roosevelt in 1945 in order to conceal the braces he wore on his legs due to a bout of polio. This panel can be opened like a tiny door, and it became a place for the children of the White House, especially President Kennedy's two kids, to play hide-and-seek.

Notes on pages 22-23:

The **Bidens' cat** is not the first cat to live in the White House—that honor goes to Tabby and Dixie, President Abraham Lincoln's cats. Lincoln's secretary of state, William Seward, gave him the two cats as a gift shortly after his election. Known to be a fan of felines, Lincoln was so fond of his cats that he often would sit and "talk" to them for long spells, especially when he was having a hard day. Lincoln once even fed Tabby from the dinner table with a fancy fork during a formal event! Mary, Lincoln's wife, was terribly embarrassed, but that didn't stop Lincoln from doting on Dixie and Tabby. He supposedly replied: "If this gold fork was good enough for [former president] Buchanan, I think it is good enough for Tabby!"

Other presidents and their families would later also bring their cats to the White House, including, famously, President Clinton ("Socks") and President George W. Bush ("India").

Notes on pages 24-25:

The **portrait of President Kennedy** that hangs in the Cross Hall outside the East Room was painted by Aaron Shikler, seven years after the president's death in 1963. The artist used old photos for models and stated that he painted the president looking down because he wanted to portray Kennedy as someone who was considerate and "a thinker."

The White House has been open to public tours since it was built. Also known as the People's House, the White House belongs to the American public—our tax dollars built it, and the president of the United States works for us, the American citizens. In 1923, under President Calvin Coolidge, tours of the White House were extended to include more rooms, and another floor was opened to the public. First Lady Jacqueline Kennedy founded the White House Historical Association in 1961 to further promote and protect the historic building and all the important artifacts inside. In a typical year, the White House has around 6,000 visitors a day—that's over a million visitors a year! The First Cat really has her work cut out for her!

SEAL OF THE FIRST CAT OF THE UNITED STATES